ABSURDIST, NIHILISTIC, AND LOVABLE,
TACKY GOBLIN **IS A VERY FUNNY**
JOURNEY THROUGH THE GROTESQUE
UNDERBELLY OF DAILY LIFE.

Fleeing a talking mold stain in the ceiling of
his bedroom in Chicago, a young man moves
to Los Angeles, where he rents an apartment
with his sister, Kim. Despite the new city, new
friends, and new love interests, something
haunts him. Perhaps Kim can help him out of
his funk. Or maybe she'll just lead him to hell…

TACKY GOBLIN

T. Sean Steele

The Unnamed Press
Los Angeles, CA

The Unnamed Press
P.O. Box 411272
Los Angeles, CA 90041

Published in North America by The Unnamed Press.

1 3 5 7 9 10 8 6 4 2

Copyright © 2018 by T. Sean Steele

ISBN: 9781944700607

Library of Congress Control Number: 2018931447

This book is distributed by Publishers Group West

Cover design & typeset by Jaya Nicely

PRAISE FOR *TACKY GOBLIN*

"*Tacky Goblin* is abruptly funny, disorienting, and—despite the ghosts, dimensional shifts, and weird demonic possessions—a totally relatable tale of ennui. Watching the lazy, deadpan narrator coast through this long chain of increasingly bizarre inconveniences is a real treat. I laughed on every page."

—Halle Butler, author of *Jillian*

"A humble comic tour de force that leads the reader through a maze of laughter and absurd, ridiculous delight. There is a wise, mordant, and beautifully crystalline vision of the universe here, and I would read a billion more chapters of this book; T. Sean Steele is a reborn Barthelme."

—Patrick Somerville, author of *The Cradle* and *The Universe in Miniature in Miniature*

"The enormous energy and the over the top subversive anarchy in *Tacky Goblin* is that of transformation. The book is a wonderful debut by a talented, comic writer."

—Stuart Dybek, author of *Paper Lantern* and *Ecstatic Cahoots*

"T. Sean Steele's *Tacky Goblin* is the future. It's also one of the most original, hilarious, inventive books I've read. Echoing the work of Richard Brautigan, Haruki Murakami, and Sam Pink, this novella presents the unending strangeness of becoming yourself. Through dog-children, black pills, and lost teeth, Steele traces the liminal moments of being lost in your twenties in LA and Chicago, and perfectly captures the travails of two siblings—brother and sister— as they negotiate the absurdities of the beginning of the twenty-first century."

—Joe Meno, author of *Marvel and a Wonder* and *Hairstyles of the Damned*

"T. Sean Steele's *Tacky Goblin* is strange but somehow comforting too, like a nightmare that you don't want to leave, or a wistful calamity. You'll love the book for its humor and absurdity, and you'll thrill at finding a new irreverent voice in fiction. Read this book. You've earned it."

—Tim Moore, Unabridged Books

"This is a deeply strange book. It's also by turns whimsical, clever, and absolutely hysterical. *Tacky Goblin* is the first book by an incredibly talented writer. Hop in on the ground floor."

—Tom Flynn, Volumes Bookcafe

"This heartfelt coming-of-age story about a boy in the dreamscape of LA wanders from one tragic hilarity to the next. Irrepressibly earnest and bold in the telling, it looks to do what we ask all good books to do: make us look again at the ordinary experiences of our lives and realize how truly extraordinary they are."

—Anthony Mangini, City Lit Books

"As anyone who has survived the gauntlet of independent adulthood knows, the transition is emotionally hard and unsettling, and as full of angst, bizarre life events, and weirdo relatives and love interests as this frothy little fantasy. The absurd plot and Steele's deadpan humor combine to make the book a delightful send-up of classic coming-of-age fiction."

—Rachel Jagareski, *Foreword Reviews*

To KJ

TACKY GOBLIN

BED-RIDDEN

I wasn't sure when I last left my bedroom.

It had been raining for a long time, and the storm washed out any sense of day or night. Out my window it was always the same: dark, wet, and overcast.

I stopped leaving my room because of shin splints. A few weeks earlier (the same day my sister emailed to say she had signed the lease on our new apartment, actually), my legs had started to ache. Now I was at the point where I could barely walk, so I was spending most of my time in bed.

There was a mold spot in the corner of my ceiling above my bed. It started as a thin black line, but because of all the rain it had grown to an oval shape. Like a mouth.

When I felt myself getting nervous about moving halfway across the country, I'd lay on my bed and stare at the mold mouth while listening to the rain patter on the roof. I found this relaxing, almost like meditation. I'd get sucked into it for who knows how long, until my mom knocked on the door and said something like, "Who are you talking to?"

For the time being it was fine, but I hoped my folks took care of the mold before I came home for Christmas. By then my ceiling would be one wet, twitchy mold mouth.

TIME FOR A NEW PHONE

My sister called today to update me on the apartment.

"There's no AC, so it gets pretty hot in the living room, but otherwise it's great. They just re-painted the walls. It's small but cute. There's crown molding. I know you like crown molding."

"Great. Can't wait."

"...what did you say?"

"I said, 'Great. Can't wait.'"

"Oh. It sounded like you said, 'Fuckshitcockasshole-whorefuck.'"

"Weird."

"To be honest, every time I talk to you lately, the connection is lousy. There's a lot of static, and the sound of your breathing is, like, amplified."

"Well, I can't do anything about it now. I still have another year on my contract before I can get a new one."

"Bummer."

"Listen, I gotta split. I'm in the middle of bleaching this bit of mold off my ceiling. Talk to you later."

"Deathiscomingforyou."

"What?"

"I said, 'See you soon.'"

CONNOR IN D.C.

My friend Connor in D.C. pointed out something to me: my legs started hurting the same day my sister signed the lease on our new apartment.

"So, you know, what about the implications?" he said.

"Meaning…"

"Meaning, your legs, commonly used for transport, stopped working the day you got an apartment halfway across the country. Your body is shutting down, preventing you from moving."

"I'm not going to walk to Los Angeles, Connor. I'm driving."

"It's symbolic. Your body is trying to tell you something."

I thought: whatever. Thanks for the insight, but I'll take it with a grain of salt, or I would if I could walk to the kitchen.

MOLD MOUTH AND ME

I had a weird dream about me and the mouth-shaped mold on my ceiling.

It went like this:

I was in bed, and the mold mouth said, "Wake up."

"Why?"

"There's someone in your room."

I looked around. It was dark, but empty.

"Not this room," the mold mouth said. "You're asleep right now. This is your dream room. A projection. I'm talking about your real room, in the real world. There's someone in there with you. I don't know who it is."

"Wait. You can be in my dream and the real world at the same time?"

"I'm mold. When you sleep, I drop tiny spores into your nose, which attach themselves to your brain. I've got a private line to your unconscious. But let's focus on the drooling stranger in your room."

"Drooling?"

"He's getting slobber all over your face. Know anybody like that?"

"No." I tried to wake up.

"Hmm," the mold mouth said. "He's kind of on top of you now. I can't see what he's doing, but..."

"But what?"

"I think his chest popped open. As in, his ribcage split in two. Kind of looks like a mouth. Like me. Except I don't have teeth."

I had just enough time to picture a gaping chest lined with teeth made of ribs when a clap of thunder woke me.

There was no one else in the room. A spat of rain gusted against my window. I wiped the drool off my pillow and tried to fall back asleep.

FIRST HE SPENT TWENTY MINUTES SHAVING THEM

"It seems to me that your legs hurt because they don't want to move to Los Angeles," the doctor said. "They're trying to prevent you from leaving."

"You're kidding me."

"It happens."

"How?"

"Well. Did you talk about the trip when your legs were in the room?"

"What?"

"They had to find out somehow."

"OK. Great medical opinion. I'm leaving."

"At least it's only your legs that don't want to move. It could've been worse. Could've been your liver. Or your butt."

HOPE THE NEW MOLES AREN'T CANCEROUS

My legs are fixed, because they're gone.

I woke from a nap and fell when I tried to get out of bed. My balance was off. I felt like I was a couple inches closer to the ground than usual. I rolled up my pants to find a pair of unfamiliar legs. They were hairy and as thick as tree trunks and they weren't mine.

"Looking good," the mold mouth on my ceiling said.

I flexed my toes. Muscles rippled up to my quads. "What did you do to me?"

"Well. You remember that drooling guy with the ribcage mouth? He came by last night and lurked over you again so I thought, *Enough is enough,* and swallowed him. Then I stripped him for parts and replaced your legs with his."

"You can't do that to me. They don't even match my skin tone. They're too light."

"They're an improvement, trust me. You had bad legs. Chicken legs. Lady legs. Anyway, they don't hurt anymore, do they?"

I stood slowly and walked around. They didn't hurt. In fact, I felt like I could jump through the ceiling.

"See?" the mold mouth said. "You're good to go. You've got a set of ham-hocks on you now. Some serious cannons. Choice cuts of meat."

"I got it. That's enough."

"A real pair of gams."

SO LONG

I was packing my bags when I noticed snow falling outside my window.

In the living room, my dad was getting ready for work.

"Where have you been?" he asked. "It's January."

"No, it isn't," I said. "It's September tenth. Where's mom? Where's the car?"

His shoulders sank. "She went to LA months ago and never came back."

"What are you talking about?"

He brightened. "Sometimes she'll video chat me. She's sharing the apartment with your sister."

"No she isn't," I said. "That's my apartment."

In the front window, untouched snow blanketed the entire street. But when I opened the front door and stepped onto the porch, it was summer. Mom was in the driveway, putting the last of our things in the car. She wiped her sweaty face with a forearm. Heat wavered off the roof of the car. A squirrel dashed across the dry grass and up a tree.

"Get your bags," Mom said, tugging on a baseball cap. "Let's get a move on."

I stepped back inside the threshold. Dad shrugged on his winter coat, quietly singing "The Last Word in Lonesome is Me." Through the window, I saw the street was covered in snow again, and Mom was nowhere in sight. I went to my bedroom and finished packing.

"Where are you off to?" the mold mouth on my ceiling said.

"California."

It whistled. "That ship sailed months ago, man."

"Outside is different than inside," I said. "One of them isn't real, and I think you're probably behind it. Spores in my brain."

"The winter's getting to you. You're losing it. Don't leave. You belong to me."

I slung my bag over my shoulder and returned to the living room. Dad was standing on the doormat. His boots were caked in snow.

"Can you help me shovel the driveway quick?" he asked sadly. "The car's stuck."

I took him by the shoulders and sat him down on the couch.

"Sure thing," I said. "You just sit right here and wait. I have a feeling you're not real, because you don't seem like you, but just in case—goodbye, Pops."

He brightened again. "Not real? That would explain a lot."

Outside, I put my bag in the trunk and sat behind the wheel. I wondered how long it would take for me to sneeze out all the spores the mold mouth had dropped into my brain.

"We're spending the first night in Provo, Utah," Mom said. "That's near Area 51, you know. Maybe we'll get abducted. I could handle it."

TURN-OFF

At our first stop for gas, Mom took out a roll of bills held together by a rubber band and peeled off a fifty.

"Here," she said. "Go pre-pay. I'll pump."

"Good god, Mom," I said. "How much money is that? Where is your credit card? You really shouldn't be carrying that much cash."

She snapped off the rubber band and flapped the stack of bills in my face. "Look at it. That's three inches of money right there."

At the western edge of Nebraska, the check engine light came on. We opened the car manual and it said to stop driving and go to your nearest Toyota dealer.

"I'm pretty sure we passed a sign that said NO SERVICES NEXT 100 MILES a half-hour ago," I said. Mom flicked on the wipers. Dank air seeped in through the AC. We were surrounded on all sides far as you could see by farmland. "I don't even think they can farm here," I said. "This land is full of rocks. Look at all those boulders. Who even owns this land? We're alone for miles. We're screwed."

"Hey, a turn-off," Mom said, pointing. Ahead I saw an exit for a town called Potter. "We'll find a gas station. All that whining for nothing."

24

She took the exit and almost immediately we came to what looked like a body shop on the side of the road. Five rusted-out mobile homes sat scattered behind the shop. A silhouette of a person appeared in the window of one.

As we pulled up, a heavyset young guy in a flannel shirt stepped out of the garage and watched us from beneath the awning.

"I'll go talk to him," Mom said. She got out.

I stayed in the passenger seat and watched Mom approach the guy. They talked. She pointed at the car, and he made eye contact with me. He disappeared back into the garage, then came out with a code-reader and headed over. He opened the driver's door, crouched on the gravel driveway, and plugged the code-reader in under the steering wheel.

"Turn on the ignition," he said. "Don't start it, just turn it on."

I did.

"So what do you do?" he asked me while we waited.

"I'm unemployed at the moment."

"I mean in your family. What's your job?"

"I don't know what you mean."

He reached under the steering wheel to readjust the cord. A long, raised scar snaked down the inside of his forearm. It looked like a piece of metal had been sewn under his skin.

"Is that the Zenith logo popping out under your skin, there?"

He held up his forearm, nodding.

"For instance," he said, "I'm the recorder. My sister is the signal. My dad is the outlet. And so on. So what do you do?"

"That must be a Nebraska thing. I don't know what you're talking about."

He sighed, then lifted his shirt. He had another scar on his belly. Again it was raised under the skin. This one looked like the front side of a VCR. He pushed a finger into where you'd insert a tape, and the skin flapped inward.

"We don't do anything like that," I said.

He frowned. "But how do you play the tapes? How will you know when to flip the switch?"

I looked past the guy. Where was Mom?

She was still by the garage, talking to a girl in a faded, flower print dress. The girl had a metal pole sticking out of her back where her spine ended at the base of her neck.

"Don't tell me you don't know about the switch," the guy growled.

The code-reader dinged and he looked at it. He stood up, smiling. "False alarm. There's nothing wrong. A soft code. I'll reset it so the light goes off. Car's fine."

Mom had walked over. "Great. Hey, hold on a sec." She took out her money roll and handed him a twenty. "For your trouble."

I tried to sleep the rest of the way through Nebraska.

FIRST DAY

My sister gave me a skull as a welcome gift.

"You can use it as a paperweight."

"Um. Is this a real human skull?"

"Don't be stupid. It's plastic or something."

"I don't think so. That's a real gold filling. Where did you buy this?"

"I didn't buy it so much as find it in the water heater closet. In a box. A locked box. A very locked box. It was a bitch cutting off all the barbed wire and smashing it open."

"Barbed wire?"

"Look, it's a gift! Take it, or don't. Jesus. Welcome to the apartment."

She went to her room and closed the door.

DON'T THINK I'M GOING TO MAKE MANY FRIENDS IN THE BUILDING

I met one of my neighbors, Laurie, outside the laundry room today.

"So you live in the Psycho Apartment, huh?"

"The what?" I said.

"The Psycho Apartment. There was this girl who lived there before you. She was nuts. Up all night, howling like a wolf, peeking in everyone's windows. She'd order soup online and get it delivered to her door, stacks of it, piled shoulder-high on the front step."

"Soup?"

"All kinds of soup. This whole building reeks of broth, haven't you noticed?"

It was true. I'd emptied a can of Lysol in my apartment to get rid of the smell. "Weird. When did she move out?"

"I dunno. Right before you moved in, I guess."

"...my sister's been living in my apartment for like a month now. I'm not the new tenant. I just moved in with her."

Laurie cocked her head. "Ah. Whoops. Well. Good luck with that, guy."

LARRY

I was going to look for a job today, but instead I ended up at Laurie's apartment. She handed me a little black pill.

"Take it," she said. "It'll clear out your system."

"Which system? I already have IBS."

"Don't be a pussy."

The pill tasted like a Spree. I settled back on the couch. I could already feel it working. "My brain feels carbonated," I said.

A shadow moved across the living room floor. I saw a man staring at us outside the apartment window. He was clean cut, with a doughy baby face and thin eyebrows. He smiled.

"There's a guy out there," I said. "Do you know him?"

"Oh, that's Larry. He's not real. That's another thing the pill does. It makes you see Larry."

Now he was standing behind the couch, resting his chin on my shoulder. I almost expected him to start whispering in my ear. It felt kind of nice.

"What a trip," Laurie said.

SKULLS, MAN

"Hey, Laurie," I said. "Do you ever see us as an item?"

"Sure. Once, I had this nightmare…"

"Yeah, all right. I only meant, I'm over here all the time anyway. You don't seem to have other friends."

She popped another black pill.

"The main reason we will never be an item is because you use words like 'item.' The other reason is because you're not soulful enough."

"Not soulful enough? I'm full of soul."

She shook her head. "Your eyes are dead, man. I can see straight through to the back of your skull."

Apparently I didn't have a brain, either. I had been feeling dull around the edges lately. The only thing keeping me pepped up were the black pills. Otherwise I had no energy. Case in point: the other night I had this dream where my sister's paperweight skull was hovering over me. I didn't feel panicked at all when it started sucking this purple mist out of my… eyeballs. "I think I know how to get my soul back," I said.

"Good for you," Laurie said. "We're still never going to be a thing."

NEIGHBOR

The guy upstairs wouldn't shut up. For the past week he'd been banging around up there until three a.m. each night.

"We could murder him together," my sister said. "A co-murder."

"It's like he's got cement blocks for feet," I said.

"We could use that. Bop him on the head and chuck him in the ocean. He'd sink."

"At least he's not playing guitar tonight."

"I think we should go up there when he's asleep and whisper subliminal messages in his ear, such as, 'Kill yourself.'"

On my desk, the soul-sucking skull paperweight watched us, waiting for me to fall asleep.

"I've got an idea," I said. "Let's gift him the soul-sucking skull paperweight. That'll sap his energy."

"Hey. I gave that to you."

"Yeah, but he seems like the sort of jerk who'd actually like skulls around his apartment."

TURNS OUT IT'S ONLY LEGAL IF YOU BURY THE BODY IN A NATIONAL PARK

Kim woke me up last night, all dressed in black.

"Hey. Wake up. Didn't you hear?"

"What?"

"The government shut down. We can do that co-murder now."

LARRY, PART TWO

I overdosed on Laurie's little black pills and brought Larry into reality.

"This is awful," Laurie said. "What a nightmare. I'm breaking up with you."

We were hiding behind the couch watching Larry sweep the living room. He had just dusted the end tables and the ceiling fan. He was tidying up.

"It's not so bad," I said. "He's only cleaning. He's a productive new member of reality. Larry's nothing but patient and nice, anyway. He deserves to be real."

"Wrong. Larry is great because he's fake. Make something real and it sucks. Everything's better in theory. Baths, for instance. Music festivals. This relationship."

Now Larry was sitting at the desk, on my laptop. "What is this, the Internet? This is great," he said. "The whole world's out there."

"Wait, he can talk now?" I said.

"He's a real person," Laurie said.

I stuck my finger down my throat and heaved up the contents of my stomach. Larry blinked out of existence.

"Gross," Laurie said. "You couldn't have gone to the toilet? You're cleaning it up."

NO RELATION

My sister came home with a surprise.

"I got us a dog." She set it down on the floor. It looked up at me, wiped its nose, and burped.

"That's a baby."

"Hmm?" Kim was already in the kitchen, doing dishes.

"You brought home a human baby."

She shook her head. "A dog. I got it at the pound. I named it Muggins. Her. I named *her* Muggins."

Muggins pulled off her sock and sucked on it. I picked her up and held her to the light. "Muggins is an awful name," I said. "Your name is Barb."

WEIRD DREAM

I had a dream Laurie passed away. She fell from the sky, and I barely side-stepped the impact.

"You could've tried to wake up before I hit the ground," she said, dusting herself off and picking concrete from her hair. "Or catch me."

"There was no warning. I would've tried if I knew."

"Here's your warning." She gave me the finger. Then she sneezed, collapsed in my arms, and died.

"Stop looking at me," Laurie said in the morning. "It's creepy."

I couldn't. The dream had been so vivid that some part of my unconscious was trying to convince me she was a ghost. I shook it off, but even then I had the sensation of watching a home video of someone long gone.

She put down her forkful of scrambled eggs. "I can't eat with you watching me like that."

"I'm sorry," I said.

"What, are you crying? Jesus." She brought her plate to the bed. "Here, eat this. You're all messed up." She tied her sneakers. "You should get out more. It's not healthy to only see, like, three people a day."

"I hate talking to strangers."

"You don't have to talk to anyone. Just see people, look at them. But don't be creepy about it. That's my assignment for you today. Go forth." She took her bag and left.

The cashier at the frozen yogurt shop was listing all the celebrities he'd seen that week. "Aaron Kilton, Ashley Bancroft, Jimmy Spritzer…"

"I don't know any of those people," I said.

"That's fine," he said. "That doesn't offend me. I know the truth, and the truth is they all walked through those doors right there. And you know what they ordered?" He gestured wildly with his arms. They were hairless and gray. He couldn't have been over fifteen years old. "They all ordered the same thing. Organic Dark Chocolate Fudge. Just like yourself."

"That's got to be a pretty common flavor," I said.

"You don't have to lie to me. It's a pleasure to meet you, sir." He tried to wink at me but didn't seem to know how. The muscles in his face convulsed and pinched. "On the house."

Outside, a tall blonde lady stood over Barb, where I'd tied her to the fencepost. "Very adorable," the lady said. "But you shouldn't let babies crawl around on sidewalks. It's disgusting."

"That's no baby," I said. "She's my dog."

The lady blinked. "That's a human baby."

"It's a common mistake." I handed Barb the frozen yogurt and she scooped it out with both hands and shoveled it into her mouth.

Next I went to the library where I could do some proper people-watching without having to worry about any of them trying to talk to me. I watched an old lady as she tried to eat a hotdog while hiding it behind an issue of *Esquire* magazine.

A librarian pushed her cart of books over to me. "Hey," she said. "You look bored. You ought to read a novel. It'll give you emotional highs and lows you never get in real life."

"I already have that problem."

She handed me a thick canvas book. "Here. This is a good one. It's about a guy who dreams that his girlfriend is dead, and when he wakes up he realizes how much he missed her, and how much that makes him love her more. He has the dream constantly, and for a while it's great, the feeling he gets when he wakes up, but eventually it's not enough. He imagines he'd miss her even more and love her even more if she really were dead, and so he plots to—"

"This is a notebook, not a novel," I said, flipping through the book. "It's handwritten in a purple gel pen."

She snatched it back. "It's a work in progress," she hissed. "And you can't bring dogs into a library."

I bounced Barb on my knee. "How dare you," I said. "This is a human baby."

"How was your day?" Laurie asked. She was in her nightgown, lotioning up her cracked heels and putting on socks.

"I got banned from the library. Then I bought a basketball, but I couldn't find a hoop in our neighborhood. Then I went out to the driveway just to dribble around, but the ball was dead and I didn't have a pump."

"But you actually saw some people."

"Oh, yeah. I think it worked. I really feel like I reset my emotional-relativity compass."

"Well. That's nice." She turned off the light. I fell asleep, exhausted, and dreamt nothing.

CHEAPER THAN DIAPERS

"Kim, there's a tooth on the kitchen floor," I said.

"Well, it's not mine."

I picked it up. It looked like a pebble. But no, it was a human tooth. "What did you do?" I said.

"Nothing. Maybe it was you. I'm not the weirdo who touched it." She was wringing out her shirt in the sink.

"Is your shirt soaked in blood?" I asked.

"No. Well, yes. But it's unrelated." I went to throw the tooth in the trash and almost tripped over something on the floor. Barb stared up at me, mewling. "Oh! It's a Barb tooth," Kim said. "She's growing up."

"She's like a month old." I picked her up and looked in her mouth. She had only three primaries left.

"Do we have any bleach?" Kim said.

Two guys were at the front door, explaining how they needed Barb back. It was later in the afternoon, after Kim had left to do whatever it was she did.

"Could you keep it down?" I said. "I just put her down for a nap."

One of them shifted his plastic garbage bag to the other shoulder.

"This would be a perfect time to take her," he said. "While her guard is down."

"She doesn't have a guard. She's a baby."

They blinked.

"Listen," I said, "I don't care if she's some genetic hybrid dream portal canine-baby escapee, or whatever it was you said. She's safer with me than you. Look at you guys. You're two schlubs in sweatpants with what looks like a garbage bag full of all the other hybrid dream portal canine-baby escapees."

"It's not about *her* safety," said the other.

"Are you threatening me?" I said.

"No, we're trying to help—"

"Listen, jerks. Let's talk about your safety for a minute. My sister is going to be home any minute now and she's not going to be happy to hear about this." I pointed at the bloody shirt drying on the fan next to the window. "She thinks she can salvage that shirt." In the bedroom, Barb started barking. "If you'll excuse me, I have to take her for a walk."

WE LOVE VISITORS

"Oh my god," my sister said from the hall. "I know what my life is missing."

"Friends? Stability?" I was in the bathroom, shaving. I had tried to grow a beard but it wasn't working out. It looked fake. The color was off. People didn't like looking at me, I could tell.

"A dollhouse," she said. "I'll make the whole apartment building in miniature. A figurine for each of us. And when we have people over—"

"—*if* we have people over—"

"—*when* we have people over, I'll make little figurines of them, too. I can show them the dollhouse with them inside of it. And when they leave, they can take their figurines with them, and bring them back when they come back. We can keep track of everyone in the building at all times."

"But why?"

"Fun. Safety. Boredom."

I rinsed the sink and examined my face. I was bleeding everywhere.

"Yikes," my sister said. "See, when stuff like this happens, I can draw little red marks all over your figurine's neck and face. For verisimilitude."

"Verisimilitude is important," I said.

"And, and! If someone is mean to me, or worse yet, mean to you, then I can maybe make a little figurine of them and break off their head and bury it in the playground across the street so they can never find it. And then I'll let them wander around headless for a while, embarrassing themselves by walking into walls or traffic or whatever, and then when it's way past the point of unbearable, I'll grind up the body in the garbage disposal."

"Hmm," I said.

"I'll have the dollhouse sink get clogged. I'll make it overflow with guts and blood. I'll use ketchup and mashed-up Skittles."

"Will this be part of the verisimilitude as well?"

"Sure, whatever," Kim said, walking away, cracking her knuckles, whispering to herself.

MAKING FRIENDS

"Hey, Laurie," I said. "Let's go play basketball."

"I'm busy." She was flopped on the bed, staring at the ceiling.

"Come on, it's exercise."

"I don't exercise. What you need," she said, "are some male friends." She rolled over and grabbed her phone off the bedside table. "Here. My cousin lives in LA. He's our age. I'll text him."

"Oh, Jesus," I said. "He's going to hate me."

"Probably, but so what? I hate all my friends. You still need some."

"If I make this shot," Marcus said, "you have to give me twenty bucks."

"No," I said.

I'd met Laurie's cousin at a playground down the street. When I showed up he was already there, wearing a full Ron Harper Bulls uniform.

The shot went in. "Boom! Twenty bucks."

"You're standing right next to the hoop."

"Don't be a dick."

"Sorry," I said instinctively.

Marcus pointed at me and laughed. "The joke's on you. I just hustled you. Last year, I got struck by lightning and now I can't miss a shot." He stood next to the hoop and made the same bank shot again, to demonstrate. "I was walking home one night through a field," he said, "and then *zap!* Struck by a hot bolt of lightning. I woke up an hour later in an alley. My clothes must've evaporated right off me. Anyway, now I'm a millionaire. I go around hustling chumps like you."

"I'm not giving you twenty dollars."

He narrowed his eyes at me. "Fine. But in lieu of money, I get to knuckle punch you in the funny bone."

"And then he stole my basketball," I told Laurie, massaging my arm. I was back at her apartment. She was in the exact same position as when I'd left.

"Did you have a nice time otherwise?"

"I hate you."

"You didn't tell him where I live, did you?" she asked.

KUMAIL

"I wish you wouldn't light so many candles all the time," I said. "You're going to burn this place down."

"I wish you wouldn't be such a weenus all the time," my sister said.

"What?"

"Sorry, I'm nervous. I've got a date tonight. His name is Kumail. I met him at the vet's office. Barb loved him so I figure he's a good guy."

"Barb wears diapers and barks at the refrigerator."

"Anyway, you'll meet him tonight. We're all going to a show together. A punk show. You and Laurie, me and Kumail."

Before I could complain, I tripped over a candle. Hot wax spilled on the floor.

"Don't worry about it," Kim said. "Barb will lick it up."

Kumail was a doughy, clean cut white man. He kept his hands in his pockets the whole concert, smiling like a goon. Laurie and I pulled Kim aside.

"His name's not Kumail," Laurie shouted over the music. "It's Larry."

"What a terrible name," Kim said.

"He doesn't exist," I said. "He's intangible. You can't touch him. Did you not notice?"

"I don't go for that kind of stuff."

"What, touching?"

Kim took a little black pill out of her pocket and swallowed it.

"Where'd you get that?" I asked.

"Your desk. These things are great. Like pop rocks for your brain."

"This is all because you overdosed that one time," Laurie yelled at me. "He's had a taste of reality and he wants back in."

We looked over at him. He was standing in the middle of the crowd. He pretended to sing along but I could tell he was mouthing gibberish.

We pulled him into the alley behind the venue. Laurie backed him against a dumpster.

"Leave us alone," she said.

"It's not fair," Larry said. He slid to the ground and hugged his knees. "I exist, I don't exist, I'm here, I'm gone. It's disorienting. All I want is some consistency."

"My boyfriends don't cry," Kim said.

A cold wind blew through the alley. Kim stomped her feet, shivering. We all watched the huddled, weeping Larry.

"You two go in and enjoy the show," Kim said. "I'll sit out here with Kumail and ride out my high until he blips out of existence."

As we went inside, I looked back and saw Kim sitting next to him against the dumpster, passing her hand through his head. Then she scooted over, passing her shoulder through his shoulder, her chest through his chest, her body through his body, until they occupied the same space. I was looking at a crying Larry and a sighing Kim all at once.

"Some boyfriend," she said.

PRECIOUS

"Barb spoke her first words this morning," Kim said, shaking me awake.

"You can't barge in here and wake me up like this," I said.

"Barge in where?" she said. "You sleep on a futon in my living room."

"A futon," I repeated, blinking away the sleep. I had dreamt I didn't exist, but now it was all coming back. I was in Los Angeles. I didn't have a bedroom. The full force of the past two months barreled down on me.

Kim put Barb on my chest. She cooed and drooled on my face.

"I was brushing my teeth and she climbed onto the toilet and spoke to me. I'm proud of her. She's so young."

Barb wagged her tail.

"What did she say?" I asked.

"'Help.'"

"Yikes," I said.

Kim shrugged. "Could have been worse. Could have been 'Mommy.'"

SHADOWS!

"I'm feeling rowdy," I said. "I'm looking to get into some shit."

"Oh, shut up," Laurie said. She was watching television.

We had a new upstairs neighbor, and while I had yet to see him I knew he was there because each night he made a horrible racket. It was different each time. One night it sounded like he was blowing across the mouth of a jug for an hour straight without taking a breath. Another night it was an hour of him humming into an oscillating fan. Last night, I heard what I thought was the sound of him clipping his nails for forty minutes. I'd never heard nail clipping that loud before. He must have had a lot of nails. Anyway, the noise was awful. Just quiet enough so it didn't wake Kim, and just loud enough that I couldn't help but strain to listen. I was losing my mind. I was irritable.

"Unless I'm way off the mark," I said, "I'm pretty sure he's taunting me. He's performing some kind of experiment on me."

"Usually you're pretty off the mark," Laurie said. "But by all means, kick his ass. I can't have this become another lame excuse for you to start sleeping over all the time." She turned back to the game.

I pointed at the television. "What is this, sports? Since when do you watch sports?"

"There are many different types of sports. You get that, right? For instance, this is football."

I headed for the door. "Feeling rowdy," I whispered to myself, nodding. I liked how it sounded.

"Oh, it's not me," said my upstairs neighbor. I was at his door. "It's an ambient-noise podcast."

"It sounds like death," I said. I looked him up and down. He was chubby but had rail thin, bowed legs, as if his jeans squeezed all the fat in his legs up above his waist.

"It's made by a cardiologist in Utah," he said. "It's what he listens to when he's sawing through breastplates." He smiled, and I flinched.

"Are you a surgeon?" I asked.

"Well, no."

"Then why listen to it?"

"Like you said. It sounds like death."

I had come up here wanting to punch this man, but now that I was looking at him I didn't know where I'd plant my fist. I looked at his nose, but I didn't want to hurt my hand. I tried to stir up my anger again, but it was gone.

"I also like it because it gets me all riled up," he said. "My heart starts pumping and I pace around the apartment. I want to punch the walls. I've never felt like that before. It's fantastic."

"Maybe," I said. "But it's got to stop."

He frowned and cracked his knuckles. "But why?"

"It's why I came up here. To get you to stop."

Then my face went numb, and I was on my butt on the concrete. I looked up. "Did you just punch me in the nose?"

He was squeezing his hand and wincing. "Yes. Sorry. Yes." He gritted his teeth. "Wow. That was not enjoyable," he said. "It felt like the right thing to do, like it'd been building for days, but Jesus. My hand!" He started to close the door. "I'm sorry. This was embarrassing. I won't play the podcast again."

"I took care of it," I said.

"Your face is all messed up," Laurie said. She was still watching the game. I sat down next to her. I felt really tired, but I knew if I fell asleep, she'd yell at me. I inhaled carefully. I could only breathe through one nostril.

Laurie pointed at the TV. "I don't even know what I'm watching. Who are all these guys in three-piece suits? Why are their ties so big? The game is only like one-seventh of what's happening." She turned it off, and we looked at ourselves in the screen. My face was covered in blood. "Wanna make out?" Laurie said.

RHODA

"I think we need to take Garth to the hospital," my sister said. "He's got a big hole in his belly."

"Who's Garth?" I said. I was unclogging the bathroom sink, pulling up gobs of hair tangled in green gunk. It was endless. It was the most fun I'd had in a while.

"Garth is the new upstairs neighbor."

I picked another hair-gob off my fingers and flung it into the garbage. Almost seemed like a waste to throw it away. "An actual hole?" I asked. "Like a doughnut hole?"

"No, more like a crater." She held up a little figurine. The stomach was hollowed out. "Like this."

"Tell me you didn't make those little figurines you've been talking about."

"I did, I did," she said. "I had to. He cold-clocked you."

"First off, he caught me off guard. Second, you can't just scoop out a guy's insides because he hit me. It's overkill."

"It isn't very sporting, I'll give you that. I was grinding away with a little nail file and upstairs I heard him begging someone named Rhoda to 'Please make the pain stop.' What an ugly name, Rhoda. Anyway, he hasn't said anything in a while, which makes me think he's not doing so hot. It was better when he was moaning."

I peered down the drain. It gurgled and burped hot, wet air into my face. "Let's look for some Drano in his apartment when we go up there."

"I feel like you're always in here, scrubbing or whatever," my sister said.

"Things don't just magically clean themselves," I said. "It takes steadfastness and a good eye."

"It's a lot of time in the bathroom."

Kim carried Garth down the stairs to the garage. "He's not so heavy," she said. "Although I guess he's missing, like, twenty percent of his body weight."

We took his car because he was oozing a lot. He collapsed in the back seat and asked us where we were taking him.

"Hey, Garth," Kim said. She sat in the back seat with him. His head was on her lap. "Who's Rhoda?"

"She was my counselor," he groaned. "I told her my life, my whole goddamned life, and then she died."

"How did she die?"

"Old age. She was sixty. I'd tell her about my problems, and she'd give me advice. Great advice. But now she's dead. I try to talk to her still, but it's not the same."

"Because she's dead," Kim said. "You gotta stop doing that. People will think you're nuts if you talk to yourself. You shouldn't tell anyone else that story, OK? You won't make friends in the building." She lifted the front of his shirt and looked at his wound. "Besides, what kind of advice would she give you right now? This is unprecedented in the history of forever, probably."

I pulled up to the ER entrance and turned around to look at him. His eyes were glazed over. "Listen, Garth," I said. "Kim's going to carry you to the door and hand you off, or maybe set you on the ground. Then we're gonna skedaddle. We'll park your car in the hospital lot for you, though."

"Thanks," he mumbled. "Sorry about your face."

"I think we're even, now."

We walked home along Los Feliz Boulevard.

"What is this, cold weather?" Kim said.

"It's the middle of the night."

She shivered. We were both wearing jean jackets.

"What did he mean, he told his whole life to Rhoda?" Kim asked. "I mean, what does that mean? Your whole life?"

"Maybe he kept a detailed journal."

"No thanks," Kim said. "Busy work."

Across the street, an old man grabbed at his crotch and leered at us. He said we smelled like shit, that he could smell our reek from all the way over there.

"Shut the hell up," Kim yelled. "We don't stink. Or, at least our apartment is pristine." She patted me on the back.

CHICAGO FOR THANKSGIVING

We didn't know what to do with Barb while we were away in Chicago. Laurie had disappeared without notice, and Garth still spent most of his days unconscious due to his injuries. Our bags were packed, we were ready to go, and Kim was making a last ditch effort to train Barb to open the fridge.

"It's not gonna work," I said. "She doesn't have hands."

"You look awful," Kim said. "Are you drunk? It's three in the afternoon."

"I don't like to fly." I'd been mixing those little black pills with alcohol, and the effect was incredible. I thought I might be a superhero. I had an almost uncontrollable urge to patrol the neighborhood, or sacrifice myself to save the universe.

"Stop touching your biceps and help me stuff Barb into my carry-on," Kim said.

ALL OF THEM PARENTS

Dad picked us up from the airport. He was bundled up against the cold. We could tell something was different.

"Seriously, what is going on?" Kim said. "You're trying to hide it under that big hat and scarf. Take those off." She wrestled off his winter hat, unwound the scarf. When he was bare-faced Kim recoiled and said, "I feel sick."

I leaned forward from the back seat to get a better look.

He looked like Mia Farrow in *Rosemary's Baby*.

"It's not so bad," I said. "You look cute. Does this mean Mom is going to look like Frank Sinatra?"

"Frank Sinatra? What are you talking about?" Kim said.

"Dad looks like Mia Farrow."

"No, he doesn't," she said. "He looks like you."

"What happened, Dad?" I asked.

"I don't know," he said. "I spent yesterday cleaning your bedroom of all the mold that had built up since you left, and when I was done I looked like this. I'm not too worried. It's already wearing off. My back hair is already growing back."

I was flattered. He didn't think I had back hair.

Dad and I were in my room because I wanted to see if the mold mouth really was all gone.

It really was all gone.

I had always assumed the mold mouth had ulterior motives, some master plan, but now I saw it for what it was: a patch of life that could be killed by bleach and hot water like anything else. Maybe it was never my enemy. Maybe it had been my friend.

"What about you? Are you worried now that we look the same?" Dad said.

"Why would I be worried?"

"I don't know," he said. "I might kill you and take over your life?"

Mom yelled to me from the living room. She wanted me to rub her feet and knew I could be guilted into anything. I took Dad by the shoulders and guided him into the hall. He struggled, but he was my size now. We had the same weakling body, but I'd been living in it my whole life.

"Give special attention to the bunions," I told him.

PETS

On the plane back to LA, I sat next to a lady with a dog. The dog was large and black, and its fur was wet. It lay on my feet.

"It's an emotional support dog," the lady said. "It's on the up-and-up. I have the papers."

"OK," I said. My stomach was still upset from Thanksgiving, and now I was on a plane with a dog whose saliva was seeping into my socks.

"That was a lie, just now," the lady said. "It's not an emotional support dog. There are no papers."

"OK," I said.

"What I mean is," she said, "no one's ever been able to see the dog but me. I don't even want her, but she follows me everywhere. You're the first person who's ever noticed her." She reached down to pet the dog. Her hand came back up covered in black hair. "I think she might be my dead twin."

"Your twin was a dog?"

"No, but she was run over by a car." She wiped her hand on the window, leaving a streak of slobber and fur. "Anyway, I'm sick of her. She's been following me for years. I thought she was only haunting me, but now you can see her."

"I wouldn't read into that. I have a creepy dog, too. This type of stuff always happens to me. For instance, see my legs? They're not actually my legs."

"Oh?"

"They were transplanted onto me by the mold on my ceiling. And sometimes I take these black pills that create an imaginary friend for me. And I used to have a human skull that sucked out my soul while I slept. I used it as a paperweight until I gave it to my upstairs neighbor. I could go on."

She scowled and gathered the dog onto her lap. "I think that's enough. I only wanted to talk to someone about my problems."

"You're complaining your dead twin isn't dead enough. Meanwhile, my bowels are counting down and we're stuck on a cylinder thirty thousand feet in the air. Problems are relative."

QU'EST-CE QUE C'EST?

"I broke the garbage disposal," my sister said. She turned it on to demonstrate. It sounded like a wailing child.

"How?"

"I was collecting Barb's baby teeth in a jar, but there were so many I ran out of jars." She still hadn't turned off the disposal. She looked down the drain. "Apparently, you're not supposed to put things like teeth or bones down a garbage disposal. I looked it up. Semi-solids only. Anything that's about seventy percent water or more. Like humans." She turned it off.

"So call the landlord."

"Heck no. Every time he comes over, he leaves me a new French movie to watch. They never end. I spend all day in front of my laptop but they go on and on. I don't have the time." She put a hand on my shoulder. "This is your responsibility for the day. Unclog the disposal. Pretend it's the bathroom drain. I know how you like cleaning that."

I admit, I got a little excited.

Kim frowned and put a finger on my nose. "When is your face going to heal?"

"It is healed."

"But your nose is kind of sideways."

"I look tough."

"You're tough to look at."

Laurie came by in the afternoon. I was under the sink. So far, I'd collected thirty-seven teeth from the drain.

"Where have you been?" I said. "I haven't seen you in days."

She tossed a DVD on the kitchen table. "Your sister loaned me some French movie. I think it might actually have been some kind of CCTV footage of an alley. It never ended. I got way too invested so I shut it off."

Using my pliers I wrenched another tooth out of the drain. I held it up, smiling. It looked like it was made of silver. "There are hundreds of these things in here. We're infested."

She tapped the DVD. "Listen, on second thought, I'll hold onto this until your sister gets back. I'm going to try and finish it. I must have been deep into the third act. I think I'm getting pretty good at French, too."

I got out from under the sink to say goodbye. She bit my nose. "I like the new look. You look tough."

"I know."

By the end of the afternoon the entire surface of the kitchen table was covered in silver teeth. The sun cut through the window and the teeth glinted. It seemed to me the solution wasn't to get rid of the teeth, but to buy more jars.

Barb came in from the other room and crawled up my leg. I picked her up and showed her the table. "Good girl," I said.

IT'S MY DIET

Garth had trouble sleeping on account of his injuries, so sometimes I sat with him at night. We were, in spite of everything, companions. I don't think he knew Kim was responsible for his belly, and the guilt made me more accommodating than usual.

"I've been having nightmares about Rhoda," he said. His apartment was hot, but for my sake he kept his blanket above his wound. "In the nightmare, I wake up and she's cooking me scrambled eggs for breakfast. I can smell them. Scrambled eggs are one of the few things I can eat now. I hate them but I don't have a choice. But then Rhoda comes into my room carrying a plate of my missing insides. She says she's holding onto them for safekeeping because I can't be trusted with them. Meanwhile the whole room smells like eggs." He sobbed. "I'm looking at her holding my insides and I've never been more in love with her. I realize it now, but it's too late: I love a dead woman."

"Or you just miss your insides a lot."

"I thought you'd understand, being with an older woman yourself."

"What?"

"You're going out with Laurie."

"Laurie's our age," I said, completely unsure. It had never come up. I thought hard. She looked our age. Although sometimes she wore a blazer.

I entered Laurie's apartment to find her talking with the landlord.

She held up a handful of DVDs. "Why did you give us these movies to watch? I don't think they're movies at all. They're surveillance footage of an apartment building in France."

"I own many buildings all over the world," he said. "I hand-pick my tenants to create perfect counterparts of the same building in each country. I bet you found the footage mesmerizing, no? Did it seem familiar?"

"...maybe. But why?"

He tugged at his suspenders. "Social experiments. I'm not sure what I'm looking for, or what I'll do with my findings. Sometimes you have to let science flow over you, results be damned."

Laurie turned to me. "What are you smiling about, weirdo?"

"How old are you?"

She gave me the finger. "Thirty-two. You knew this."

I moaned.

"Oh, Christ," Laurie said. "Which French guy is his counterpart?" she asked the landlord.

"The schoolboy. The one with IBS."

HO HO HO

"We're going to a Christmas party," my sister said. "Garth invited us. I tried to sneak out of the building without him noticing but he was waiting by the door again. Apparently he can't fly home because he doesn't have an abdomen, so his parents are coming here."

"Can I bring Laurie?" I said from the futon. I was examining my legs. They had begun to mildew and stink. They were decaying like the transplanted legs of a dead man they were.

"No," Kim said. "He explicitly said no one could come but us. Siblings and parents. That's what he said." She poked my calf with a finger. It left a depression. "What's wrong with your legs? They're all mildewy. Maybe you got an old person STD from Laurie. One they've been keeping a secret from us youths. Although, her legs are fine." She nodded, thinking. "Laurie has good legs."

Out of respect for Garth's lack of a digestive tract, his parents didn't make a Christmas dinner. We sat around and drank Capri Suns instead.

"The weather out here is very nice," his mom said.

"It is," his dad said. "Although my sinuses are having trouble adjusting. Nosebleeds everywhere."

I absently scratched my knee, even though I couldn't feel an itch. I was wearing gym shorts, the only things that fit. My legs were beginning to bloat.

"We should put on Christmas music," Kim said, but his mom smiled and politely gestured for her to be quiet.

"Garth tells us you all spend a lot of time together," his dad said. "That you're great friends."

"Not really," Kim said, opening another Capri Sun.

Garth shifted uncomfortably in his chair, but then, he did that all the time.

"All the siblings in one room," his dad said.

"It's just that he talks about you so much," his mom said carefully. "It's like we know you. Like you're our own kids."

"Yikes," Kim said.

His parents looked at each other. "We want you to know that we think of you as our own, that's all," his dad said. "We'd like you to think the same of us."

"What the hell, Garth," I said.

"You two helped me through a rough time," Garth said. "I only wanted to repay the favor. My parents are the best parents in the world." He smiled. "Merry Christmas."

His dad leaned forward and put his hand on my knee. "Obviously it gets a bit dicey with you still having birth parents. You'd have to do some renunciations."

"You people are all mixed-up," Kim said, standing. "Our parents could kick your asses. *I'm* about to kick your asses." She pointed at Garth's dad. "Seriously, nosebleeds? Who wants a dad that gets nosebleeds?"

He lifted his hand away from my knee and with it came a large swatch of dead skin. He gagged.

"Let's get out of here," Kim said, heading for the door. "I've got some figurines to mutilate."

"Right on. But you need to carry me," I whispered. "I can't feel my legs."

CHICAGO

We were at a bar in our hometown of La Grange. It was the night before New Year's Eve, and everyone we knew from high school was crammed inside. Somehow it was still freezing. I couldn't for the life of me remember what time we'd arrived, or why we'd come, but now that we were here it seemed like a good idea to keep drinking.

"How are your legs?" Kim asked.

"I showed them to Mom and she said the problem is psychosomatic."

"But they're visibly rotting."

"That's what I said, but she thought I was joking. To her they look like normal legs. She made me think I was delusional."

"You're not. I can see them. But they really feel better? You can walk normally again?"

I shrugged. This was boring. I didn't like explaining my problems. My legs worked or they didn't. Who cared? The facts existed, or they didn't, whether or not I paid attention to them.

My sister sighed. We were sitting at a corner table, surveying the room. "I'm going to either mingle or rumble," she said. "But I won't know which until I talk to someone."

"I'd bet on the latter," I said.

"You should consider optimism in the new year."

"That was optimism."

She pretended to wave to someone and walked into the crowd.

BACK IN LA

"Happy fucking New Year," I said. "Laurie dumped me."

Kim barely looked up. "What happened?"

"The landlord offered to let her swap apartments with her counterpart in his building in France. She took him up on it because the days were going by faster and faster but she wasn't getting any closer to the future she imagined for herself. Or something. I don't know. I didn't factor into any of it."

Kim shrugged. "Don't obsess. She was a grown woman, and you're a child. This was inevitable."

"I'm fine. I just need a big meal. A big steak with a lot of salt. And a bottle of whiskey. Also, I'd like to take a bath."

"Why?"

"I've read that's the proper response to heartbreak."

"You're not heartbroken, you're stunned. There's a difference. You don't have enough feelings to be heartbroken. Anyway, the steak-whiskey-bath thing sounds like some he-man bullshit. I started re-reading *Catcher in the Rye* the other day but had to stop because Holden reminded me too much of you."

"But he's a teenager."

"Mmm-hmm."

I flopped down on my futon. "I hope my next girlfriend lives in the same apartment building as us again. That was super convenient."

71

PITY PARTY

It was the middle of the night and upstairs Garth was having loud, raucous sex. They'd crossed the half-hour mark.

"Do you hear that?" Kim called from her bedroom. "Listen to that. What is this, the theatre?"

"This is awful," I said.

"If my figurines had genitalia I would deal with this," she said. "As it is, I might have to chop him off below the waist."

I didn't think that would accomplish anything. We'd deal with one thing, and something else would sprout up to take its place. Maybe we could change people, but we couldn't change our situation. Annoying things were always happening to us. I said as much to Kim.

"That was the most pathetic speech I've ever heard," she said. "You've really got to get over the Laurie thing. This is your last night to be sad about it. Then it's over, never to be spoken of again. Got it?"

We were silent for a minute. Garth didn't seem to be in any hurry to wrap things up.

"Don't think of it as annoying," Kim said. "Think of it as stimulation. Getting your ire up to face another day. That's what I do."

IF IT'S YELLOW

I'd taken a certain complaint out of rotation months ago because it was always met with an eye roll or an unconvincing assurance that things would change, that she'd really remember next time. But today I opened the bathroom window and got a whiff of fresh air and realized I didn't have to accept things for the way they were. I didn't have to live like this.

"You've really, really got to start flushing the toilet," I told Kim.

"Don't you know there's a drought?"

"No."

"I sent you an email about it," she said.

"An email…"

"Yeah! An email!"

"I haven't been online in a while. Like a week."

"Why not?"

"You know. Everyone is always trying to contact me. It makes me nervous."

"Jesus Christ," she said. "I try so hard to keep you on an even keel, but it can't all be on me. You have to help me out a little."

"Don't try to trick me," I said. "We were talking about how you don't flush the toilet."

"I mean, of course there's a drought. People still have automatic sprinklers going. In January! Humans are disgusting."

"The toilet is disgusting. What if I told everyone you don't flush?"

"Trust me, this is only interesting to you."

"Oh, we'll see about that," I said. "We will see about that."

THERE ARE PEOPLE INSIDE

Kim didn't like when I called her at work, but this time I had to. I tried to start the conversation off on a good note.

"You have one of those nice telephone voices," I said. "It's a shame about text messaging. You were born in the wrong era."

"Look, I'm busy trying to keep a two-year-old from accidentally committing suicide," she said. "What do you want?"

"I locked myself out of the apartment."

"How?"

"I'm not sure. I went to the laundry room and then I came back and the door was locked."

"This is why you need a day job, so we don't have incidents like this."

"Let's focus on the task at—" I stopped. There was a sound coming from inside the apartment.

"What?" Kim said.

"I hear voices in there," I said. "A man and a woman. I think they're bickering. What should I do?"

"Try knocking," she said.

A man sat at our kitchen table glowering at his plate and complaining about the food. His hair was slicked back with Brylcreem. He tugged at his grease-stained wife beater. "This steak is moldy," he said.

"Don't be melodramatic," said his wife, who had introduced herself at the door as Susan.

"There's a worm in it." He jabbed at the steak with his fork. "It's like this food has been sitting out for decades. Learn to cook." He choked down a piece anyway.

Susan rolled her eyes and tied her apron. "We're not usually so out of sorts," she told me. "Normally I'd say we'll get it together, but I'm having a premonition that today ends in pieces." The tendons in her neck kept twitching. She picked up a knife.

"I think there's been some confusion," I said.

"Goddamn right, confusion!" said the husband, dropping his fork in disgust. "The food tastes awful, my clothes are moth-eaten, and I have a horrible ache in my chest. We don't have time for visitors."

"You're the visitors," I said. "I live here."

He pounded his fist on the table. "Don't give me that! We've lived here for nearly ten years. I remember, it was the day FDR died. What, are you the landlord's son? Is this some kind of scheme? Do you want to get throttled?" Before I could answer, he got distracted scratching his chest. He started to pull off his shirt. It practically crumbled away. He examined his chest, but there was nothing there. "I thought I felt something," he mumbled. Susan looked back and forth between her knife and his chest.

76

I knew what was happening. "I get it," I said. "You're haunting me. A horrible thing happened here, and you're operating on repeat."

"Horrible?" Susan said. "Try wonderful. I couldn't stand this man. Every day I dreamt about plunging this knife into his chest. And now every day I get to. This might be heaven." She laughed too hard.

"Hasn't this gone on long enough?" her husband asked. "You've been killing me every day for decades, way longer than we were ever together alive. It isn't fair."

"Oh, quit whining," she said. "You get your licks in, too." She turned to the side, and I saw she had a fork sticking out the back of her head. "I'm sorry," she told me. "I'm being a terrible host, but you're the first guest we've ever had."

"That's OK. I don't think I'm supposed to be here, anyway."

"Could you lock the door on your way out?"

As I left I saw her advancing on her husband, who'd become preoccupied with his steak again.

I sat on the steps and waited for my sister to get home.

"I hate this place," I told Kim. "I hate the landlord. First he ships my girlfriend off to France, then it turns out he's renting us a haunted apartment. I sleep in the same room where two people got killed. No wonder I'm losing it."

"You're losing it because of your diet. You have to eat better. You're eating a box of Mike and Ikes a day. It's like you're building a cardboard nest under your futon."

"No, I think I'm losing it because of the ghosts killing each other in perpetuity."

In the kitchen we heard silverware clatter to the floor, but when we checked, nothing was out of place.

"Maybe we can get the rent lowered," Kim said.

HOMELESS

"Let's open a joint checking account," I told my sister.

"No."

"Then let me borrow eighty bucks."

"What for?"

"I cannot for the life of me remember to move my car for street cleaning." I had just received my third parking ticket in three weeks.

"Just set an alarm, idiot."

The truth was, I had chosen not to move my car. On street-cleaning day, I'd wait until five minutes past noon, then rush outside in my shorts and berate the parking official writing the ticket. I'd unload a week's worth of frustration. I'd never been so mean to anybody in my life. It was fantastic. Of course, the downside was I was hemorrhaging money.

"What you need is a day job."

"Stop saying that."

"Then you wouldn't be struggling to leave the apartment by noon."

"A day job…" I said. "That's not really… I have to keep the apartment tidy… and I like to read books. I don't have time to… you know…"

She shoved me out the door. "Don't come back until you're employed."

HIATUS

"Where the heck have you been?" my sister asked.

"I was applying for jobs," I said.

"For a month and a half?"

"What? No. Like a couple of hours."

"I thought you were dead," she said. "I even called the cops. There was an investigation and everything. I was their primary suspect. I spent two days in a holding cell."

"I don't know what you're talking about. I was gone for an afternoon. You kicked me out and said, 'Don't come back 'til you find a job.'"

"Did you?"

In truth, I'd spent the afternoon at the library, killing time reading comic books. "That's not the point," I said. "You're telling me I somehow lost thirty-five days in a few hours?" I sat on my futon. "Did I miss anything?"

"Sure did. I got pretty jacked. I can do one hundred push-ups in a row now." She flexed a bicep. "Also Laurie came back looking for you. She stuck around for a couple of days but then sort of gave up on you. I let her stay here. Dude, did you know she only wears sexy lingerie to bed? Even I was getting hot and bothered."

I handed Kim a pillow. "Please smother me to death."

She patted me on the head. "You can't kill anybody with a pillow, you dope. Believe me, I've tried."

INCENSED

"This place reeks of incense," my sister said.

"I've been feeling aggressive lately," I said. "I'm trying to calm down."

"Well, yeah. You've got a month's worth of emotions to catch up on. Have you tried cleaning the bathroom? That usually helps you relax."

The bathroom was as clean as it was going to get. I'd re-caulked the tub and the toilet, and spent the early afternoon tweezing goop out of the sink drain. Nothing helped.

Kim sniffed the air. "This smells familiar. Where'd you buy it?"

"I didn't. I pilfered it from a wooden chest with a lock. A busted lock. From your closet."

"My artillery chest?" She smacked me across the back of the head. "You idiot. That's special incense. It doesn't calm you down. It amplifies your mood."

"Well, shit." I went to my closet and dug around. "I guess it's time to put all this aggression to good use."

"Oh, no."

"Oh, yes." I tossed her my basketball. "We're hitting the courts. I'll loan you a tank top."

We went to the Poinsettia Community Center and played two-on-two against two teenagers who looked exactly alike.

"Twins?"

"No, asshole," they said. "I'm the Multiple Man." One of them blew by me for an easy lay up.

"We're losing," Kim said. "Badly."

"It's hard to keep track of who's guarding who," I said. "You're basically cheating."

"At least I didn't drag my sister to play with me," they said. "She doesn't even want to be here."

"Yes, I do," she said.

"No, you don't," they said. "You're five-two."

"Five-four!" She bounced the ball off one of their faces. They both collapsed to the ground, clutching their noses. Kim looked at me. "Wow. I thought he was kidding about the Multiple Man thing. Should we take one of them home, for experiments?"

"Please, not again," they said. "We're the only two left."

I OUGHT TO START
CARRYING MY OWN ROLL

"How's work?" I asked my sister on the phone.

"It's been a shit day, little brother. I thought Barb might like to meet the boy, so I took them both to the park. But she got too attached. When it was time to go, she snatched him in her teeth and hopped the fence. I followed them to the reservoir. They ducked under the spillway. Underground. It's good you called now. I have to go after them and I bet I'll lose my signal down there."

"So you won't be home at the regular time?"

"No, I'll probably get lost in the tunnels. Why?"

"I have a hot date tonight and I need help getting ready." My neck hair wasn't going to shave itself.

"With who?"

"A girl I met at the occult shop around the corner. I was buying incense."

"You really should just go to Bed Bath and Beyond. Somewhere more your speed," she said. "Also, put the razor down. Remember what happened the last time you tried to shave your own neck hair? No one made eye contact with you for weeks."

The date was a bust. She only wanted me for my body, to host a demon who would then impregnate her with hellspawn. Or something. I had trouble paying attention. She'd tied me up in her basement.

"Don't you have any of those nice waxy ropes? These ones are rubbing me raw," I said. "You might as well be using duct tape."

"I don't buy duct tape," she said as she approached with a ceremonial knife. "I can't stand the sound when you peel it off the roll. Now, be quiet. I need to concentrate."

"Look, lady. My soul's been ripped out and put back in a dozen times over. I'm chock full of corpse bones. I'm damaged goods. This isn't going to work."

"Have some self-confidence," she said, and sliced open her palm.

The next morning I sat on the sink while Kim wrangled a muck-covered Barb into the bath.

"I'm fine," I said. "It didn't take. The demon only half-possessed me. The worst he can do is whisper horrible, suggestive things in the back of my head. But I'm like, get in line, buddy."

"So did you impregnate her?" Kim asked.

"Oh, no. She cut me too deep. I lost a lot of blood. She ended up giving me a lift to the ER."

"Good to hear. Things went OK on my end, too. They didn't get deep into the tunnels. They got distracted playing fetch with a dead rat. Barb has a pretty decent throwing arm."

The sun dipped below the window frame, its light glinting off the edge of the tub. The pipes in the wall creaked. The faucet sputtered and its flow became a deep red. Barb sighed with pleasure as Kim dumped a cup of warm blood over her coat. I blinked and it was water again.

"It's just one thing after another, isn't it?" I said.

"Preach," Kim said. "But really, you should've known this girl had ulterior motives. Look at your neck. No harmless girl wants a guy with a thicket back there."

BORING AND STUPID

Something was wrong with the bathroom mirror. My reflection was a lot better-looking than me. He knew how to shave without goring his neck. Also, it looked like he actually paid someone to cut his hair.

"They're called barbers," Kim said. "And he's a chump for going to one. Your hair looks fine. I do a good job considering we don't have clippers. Or scissors."

My reflection blinked at us. I pretended to pick my nose as an experiment. He mimicked me, but I could tell his heart wasn't in it.

"Maybe it's that demon the occult lady planted in the back of your head," Kim said. "He's perfect-looking, which is a sure sign of evil. There's a way to defeat this sort of thing. I saw it in a movie. You've got to set up a bunch of mirrors so they're reflecting off each other. You confuse him, trap him in one, and then break it. Or something like that. I don't remember. The movie was boring."

"This is the only mirror we have," I said. "Anyway, I kind of like looking at him. He boosts my confidence."

"Fine, whatever." She left the bathroom. "But this is exactly how that stupid movie started."

"He's got very nice lips," I said.

LOOSEY-GOOSEY

And now Kim was getting ready for her own date. Supposedly this guy was a real person, even. She said he knew all about tangibility and human bodies.

"He asked if I knew how people lost weight," she said, brushing her teeth. "Do you know?"

"You poop it out," I said.

"You breathe it out of your mouth. It made me think of that demon the occult girl spawned inside of you. You know the one. That demon?"

"Yes, I know it."

"Maybe you should just breathe a lot and it'll vacate the premises. You know, hyperventilate?"

She stood there, waiting for me to start hyperventilating.

"No, I don't want to," I said.

"Why not?"

"I can't right now. It's not a good time for me." I was just saying no in different ways. "No, no thanks. It's not for me." •

The more ways I said no, the grumpier Kim became. She spat into the sink.

"I feel sick," she said. "What if he frontloaded all his good conversation?"

"The poop stuff?"

"There wasn't any poop stuff. You brought up the poop stuff. I mean the breathing. He's got nothing left on breathing and now he's going to talk about his family. He'll give me details about his family, and then he'll expect details about my family. I don't know any details about my family."

"Oh, sure you do," I said.

"Do I? Do I, really?"

"Oh, sure. You can at least list your family members, can't you? Just list them out. There's me, and, and… I mean, the other thing is, maybe he won't talk about family at all."

She spat into the sink again. "What, he's going to talk about his family and I'm supposed to pay attention? How do we keep finding ourselves in these insane situations?"

I opened the medicine cabinet and selected a pill bottle.

"What are those?"

"My anxiety meds. You can have them."

"I didn't know you took pills. Gimme." She snatched the bottle and read the label. "These aren't anxiety pills," she said. "They're anti-diarrheals."

HOT NIGHT

We were making up stories about people we'd killed. It was Kim's turn. She described a Purple Heart veteran who bet she couldn't find his scar. When she failed, she produced an old-fashioned straight razor and made her own, waving the blade in front of his neck, which split into a red oval. He opened his mouth, and before it filled with blood she saw the scar. A bullet hole in the back of the throat.

"I don't understand this game," said Rick, my friend from high school. He was staying with us indefinitely.

"It keeps your mind sharp," said Kim. "Like Sudoku."

Rick lay back on the cot we had set up next to the kitchen table. Moonlight through the blinds softened against his face. He looked like an angel.

"I push a stockbroker in front of an eighteen-wheeler," he said. "The tires rip off his thousand-dollar three-piece suit and mulch his face into ground beef. Bystanders cheer. His keepers bury him in a porcelain Venetian mask, but I steal it before they close the casket. On the one-year anniversary of his death, I fill it with raw hamburger meat and leave it on his widow's doorstep."

"Poetry," said Kim.

IS THAT A PROMISE?

Kim tweezed a splinter from her heel but it kept coming. It wasn't a splinter at all but an infinite strand of hair. She spooled it around her hand and kept pulling. I briefly wondered if hair was all she had inside her body, like if she continued her body might flatten into a rug. But she said she could feel it tugging at the inside of her head, like an ingrown hair from her scalp that had rooted its way along her skull, twisted around her spine, her hip, and wound down her Achilles tendon until it poked out through the bottom of her foot. She stopped pulling and looked up at me and Rick. "What a shame if it snapped," she said. The spool glistened; maybe the inside of the body was the ultimate shampoo. I'd recently ditched my shoulder-length hair for a crew cut, and while looking at the spool I felt an inordinate sense of loss.

"It seems disrespectful to snap it," Kim said.

"Disrespectful to who?"

"Time."

"Tie it in a bow around your foot," Rick said.

"I'll limp."

"Shove it back up into your heel," I said.

"Unrealistic."

Finally, it had to be done. She pinched the hair near the base of her foot and yanked. She went cross-eyed as it plucked away from the inside of her scalp. She finished pulling and dumped the spool in the trash. "This stays in the trash. If I find either of you wearing it as a necklace or whatever, I'll make you eat it."

Our eyes twinkled.

LONELY AUGUST

Rick was out of town and Kim was going back to Chicago for a month. The day before she left she filled the refrigerator with a hundred dollars' worth of groceries.

"Unnecessary," I said.

"You have a tendency to wither away when left alone. You forget to eat."

"Untrue," I said.

"Remember when I went to San Francisco for a week? I came home and the fridge was empty. You were surviving on pickles you got from work. Your mouth was full of canker sores."

"Unrelated," I said.

I was sick of people thinking I couldn't take care of myself. I wanted to be a strong, independent person. I wanted to be decisive and assured. I wanted to be a beacon of strength, a pillar of wisdom on which all my family and friends could lean.

Kim clapped her hands in front of my face and I snapped back to the present. "This is exactly what I'm talking about." She wheeled her luggage to the door. "I asked Garth to check on you periodically."

"Garth is checking on *me?* He can't even go to the bathroom without help."

"He has trouble with stairs, too. He says he'll knock on his floor every night until you shout back, 'Good night sweet angel best friend.' He insisted on choosing the code sentence so he'll know it's really you."

"Oh, I'll respond with something." I rummaged in the closet for our figurine collection. "He'll know it's me."

BEDTIME

In protest of her absence, Barb wouldn't come out from under Kim's bed. By day two the situation had escalated into a hunger strike and I had to crawl in after her.

"It was incredible," I told Kim on the phone. "Have you ever been under your bed? It felt like I'd crawled into a tremendous cavern, except when I rolled onto my back the night sky stretched endlessly above me. There were stars and comets and unknown planets, and moving among the constellations were all my regrets and faults and mistakes I wasn't even aware I had made. Looking into the sky, I found myself completely empty, and I knew I would be empty forevermore because the aforementioned regrets and faults and mistakes I wasn't even aware I had made were the soil from which all that I had been and could be grew. Basically, the contents of my self were floating away into space and I watched non-existence accept me back into its arms."

"The contents of my self were floating today, too," Kim said. "Then I flushed. But to answer your question: no, I haven't been under my bed because it's impossible. I sleep on a mattress on the floor. What happened is, the bed ate you. I told you to stay out of my room. All the evil shit in there is my burden. You can't handle it. Did you get Barb back, at least?"

"No, I think she's lost forever. I'm still under here, actually. I just called because I wanted someone to talk to."

"Well, good," she said. "As long as you're talking to someone you'll probably continue to exist. Don't hang up."

But I struggled for anything to say.

"I'm at home in La Grange for the weekend," Kim said, picking up the slack. "I'm in the kitchen right now, looking in the refrigerator. I'd forgotten what a full fridge looks like. It, too, is incredible. Do you want me to describe it to you?"

"Yes, please," I said.

IMPROV

I sat in front of my laptop and watched the backs of my hands glisten with sweat. I was trying to write a story, but it was clear to me the heat had sapped my creative energies.

"Rick," I said, "give me a title. Any title at all, and I'll build a story around it."

"'Pussyfinger.'"

I closed my laptop. "We need to get out of here."

"I'm real homesick," Rick said from his cot. He was leaning against the window fan. "I miss my mom."

"You miss air conditioning."

We ended up at a Men's Warehouse in Glendale. Rick's uncle, a movie composer, had given us two extra tickets to the Emmys and we needed to get fitted for tuxes. An old man wrapped measuring tape around my chest. He was a lot shorter than me, and when I looked down I saw beads of sweat quivering atop his scalp.

Meanwhile Rick sat at a desk across from a younger salesman. "No flowers, no vests. We'll need cufflinks. Bow ties. No shoes; we already have those. We want a real clean look. Slim fit. Class. We're going to the Emmys, you know."

"Are you nominated?"

"Not this year."

I was anxious to leave. We'd parked in the Trader Joe's lot across the street and I didn't want to get towed. Trader Joe's, Men's Warehouse, Emmys. A lot of brand names in one day for me. The upside of being cooped up in the apartment all day was that I had forgotten these places existed. I was a little overwhelmed. I felt like an idiot.

The old man measured my chest again. He looked at me. "Stop breathing so heavily. Your rib cage keeps changing size."

By the time we got home it was cooler outside the apartment than in, so we spent the early evening drinking beer on the front steps. We listened as next door a mother yelled at her daughter.

"You need to start behaving like an adult," the mother said.

"I'm five!"

Rick opened another beer. Luckily he'd brought out the bottle opener. I was pretty sure I'd locked us out of the apartment and I didn't want to deal with it just yet.

"I feel a lot better," Rick said. "What I'm realizing is the solution to so many emotional problems is to simply ride them out."

"Sounds like you don't really have emotional problems."

"Even better."

KEYSHAWN? DIJON?

I picked up Kim from LAX. She had pink hair.

"I don't want to talk about it." She threw her luggage into the back seat and climbed in after it.

"This isn't a taxi service," I said. "You have to sit up front."

"I'll sit where I want. Come on, drive. They're honking at you. You hate being honked at."

But I didn't move. Neither did Kim. She straightened in her seat, recognizing a standoff. Her eyes said, 'I live for this,' but I was ready.

We would go on sitting there for the next five minutes, until airport security tapped on my window.

During those five minutes, I could feel the situation ballooning into something unfamiliar, and I had a vague sense I would be manhandled at the end of it, but I had been in Los Angeles for nearly a year and I needed to take a stand on something.

The honking continued. A bus nearly sideswiped us. I looked at Kim in the rearview.

"None of my clothes fit anymore," I said. "I'm shrinking."

"They're going to put you in a small, windowless room," she said. "They're going to ask you so many questions you won't even remember your own name."

"I like Bob Hope Airport more," I said. "It's small and quiet and yellowing, like a retirement home. Most people hate retirement homes, but it's a mistake to follow your gut instinct. You have to dig deeper. Like, nobody honks at you at retirement homes."

"That was fun," she said, as a knuckle rapped against the glass.

HOLD STEADY

Kim's car was in the shop getting a new radiator so I had to pick her up from work. I was nervous because they'd cut up my license at the airport but she told me not to be a baby. Her license went missing years ago and she was doing fine. "A driver's license is one of those things people say you need but really you don't. Like bedsheets, or protein." I asked how she bought alcohol.

"Who buys alcohol? I've never paid for a drink in my life."

And so at midnight I met her at the curb along the Silver Lake Reservoir, at the bottom of the long, winding driveway of the house where she worked as a nanny.

"What's wrong with the roof of your car?" she asked as she got in. "It's all scraped up."

"High schoolers," was all I said. It was enough. She nodded knowingly. High schoolers were Kim's least favorite thing and I tossed the blame at them whenever possible.

"Did they try to talk to you?" she asked.

"No. I kept away until they left."

"Good. Never let them talk to you. They're skinny and they tell a lot of inside jokes and make you feel bad for not understanding even though you don't really care anyway. I don't like to generalize, but in this case it's true for all of them. Plus, sometimes they sneak into college parties and trick you into kissing them. Not that it's happened to me, but you hear things."

I put the car in drive. Actually, I'd spent the evening carrying all of our furniture out of the apartment, holding it steady on the roof of the car with one hand, and dropping off our tables, desks, chairs, and bookshelves at street corners around the neighborhood. We were moving back to Chicago at the end of the month, and Kim had tasked me with selling everything on Craigslist. But I'd never made an account on the Internet for anything and I wasn't going to start now.

Kim leaned her head against the window and looked out at the reservoir. Our kitchen table was coming up at the next corner but she didn't notice it.

"What a goddamned day," she said. "Do you ever feel like you've lost sight of what it's all about?"

"Oh, all the time. I'm not sure I ever knew in the first place."

"I just wish I knew how to fix the misery. Maybe it's you. Maybe you're the problem."

This didn't offend me. This was standard postwork behavior. I drove past our couch, which I'd put in the same spot I'd found it six months ago.

At the apartment she was surprised to see I'd gotten rid of all our stuff so fast. I made up a story about a guy with a dust fetish who bought it all in one fell swoop. She asked how much I charged for everything and I realized where I'd gone wrong.

"Uh, thirty bucks. I discounted him for taking it all."

"You idiot. We basically got robbed and you just watched it happen."

She held out her hand for the money. I opened my wallet.

"Whoops," I said. "Looks like he short-changed me a bit."

RETCON: I HAVE FRIENDS

We were playing Twenty Questions in the car on the way home from San Francisco. I hated games but I was trying to be a more open-hearted person during these, my last days in California.

"Is it a human being?" Alec asked, half-asleep in the backseat.

"Yes," I said.

"Is it you?" Jeannette asked. She was driving.

"...yes."

We entered the city limits. The sky was pink with pollution to the west, but for a moment the sun broke through the haze, glaring off the windshield, a blinding white. After it passed, I turned in my seat and studied Alec, who by now had fallen asleep. Generally speaking, Alec was always asleep. I was too high-strung to ever sleep in public and almost admired him for it. His glasses slipped down his nose and I pushed them back up. I pressed two fingers against his lips.

"Thanks for inviting me to come with this weekend," I told Jeannette.

"We had to fight to get you to go. After you said no, we spent a week strategizing to get you to change your mind."

"No, you didn't," I said. "I'm my own man."

She patted my shoulder. "You're our little marionette."

"You sound like my sister."

"Maybe because we both understand there's a default way to talk to mopes like you. Anyway, remember all your suicide jokes? And how uncomfortable they made everybody? Who put an end to those?"

"People loved those jokes," I said.

"Sure they did," she said. "That's why we're your only friends."

A half-truth. Certainly there were other people who considered themselves my friends, even if I didn't reciprocate. Garth, for example. For guys like that, a half-friendship was as good as it was ever going to get. I wondered if he knew it, and my heart thumped with sadness for him and the rest of his long, long life. It was truly the least I could do.

"If I'm your puppet," I said, "then how come I'm choosing to move across the country?"

"Exactly," Jeannette said.

We rolled along in silence in the carpool lane, then crossed three lanes of traffic to exit the 101. As we turned left onto Hollywood, Alec began to snore in staccato gasps. I turned around and knuckled him in the sternum until he stopped.

SMOTHER BROTHER

We were picking the last bits of double-sided tape off the walls, and it was this that finally broke us.

"Insane asylums have the right idea," Kim said.

"Absolutely, absolutely, absolutely."

"Clean lines, white walls. No decorations, no distractions. Pure life of the mind. What were we thinking, putting things on the walls? Do either of us even like *Fargo* that much? How did that poster get up there? And who used twenty pieces of tape to hang it? We were reckless. No thought for the future."

I scratched my thumbnail at the corner of some tape, and though it felt like scraping a chalkboard, I kept doing it over and over until my spine stopped convulsing in protest, until I accepted the irritation as part of my being. It no longer grated me because I had become the nails on the chalkboard, the knife against the plate. I was on all your goddamned walls.

"And frankly, I don't see a future where these get cleaned," Kim said. She slumped to the floor. "Maybe if we leave some hangers in the closet and a couple of pairs of shoes by the door, they'll consider it a fair swap and we'll still get our security deposit back. Dibs on the hangers. You give the shoes."

I kept scratching. It was shockingly easy to be something hated. You rode the tide of the hate—no, "rode" implies effort. It swept you up and kept you going. The wall went soft like wet putty against my thumbnail, and maybe I was about to be absorbed into the plaster, to become one of those arms that reach out of the wall at night and torment the tenant à la *Repulsion*, but then I realized I had only burst a blister. I slumped down the wall next to Kim, exhausted.

"Let's maintain a severe aesthetic at our next apartment," she said. "No posters, nothing. Maybe some nice rugs. That could be our thing. Rugs. Except then we'd need a vacuum."

Kim held out her own fingers, also swollen red.

"Listen to this," she said. "I was talking to Mom on the phone today and she called me neurotic. My own mother. It's like no one can see the reason I'm neurotic is because I'm trying really, really hard not to be evil. You can see that, can't you? Can't you?"

"I don't think you're evil," I said.

"Of course you don't. You worship me. It's disgusting."

"No, I don't."

"Bullshit. I wake up every morning with a mug and a fresh pot of coffee steaming on my end table."

"I refuse to feel defensive about that."

She stood up to continue picking at tape. I hoped this meant she forgot about giving away my shoes.

MAN TO MAN

I was back in Chicago, but Kim was still in Los Angeles for another month. Alec was letting her stay in his basement room at a house in Echo Park while he crashed at his girlfriend Jeannette's. Friends crashing at friends' places, building communities, hustling apartments and jobs, everyone working together to get their shit together. Meanwhile I was prostrate on the couch at my parents' house doing none of those things.

"Who drank all my Rumchata?" Dad asked from the kitchen. "I bought it yesterday."

"'Twas your son."

"Don't lie to me. Kim's in LA." He sat down on the sofa across from me and began to describe, play-by-play, his lunch hour basketball game. I breathed into the cushion until my face began to sweat.

"Remember all those blood smears we saw along the interstate, from Flagstaff all the way to Quincy?" I said. "Sprays of gore, like an animal had been hit and dragged under a car for twenty feet until it released and thumped down the shoulder, a hundred times over? I was wondering, does the state have someone rinse that shit away, or do they let the rain take care of it?"

"I didn't see any of that. You were hallucinating."

"But there were so many of them. To hallucinate that much carnage, you'd have to have something really wrong with you." I sat up. I ought to have been used to hallucinations by now, but a small, tired, innocent part of me had hoped a cross-country road trip might somehow shift my life into a different genre. "I mean, isn't it equally possible you hallucinated there weren't any blood smears? Isn't it?"

My dad settled back in his seat.

"Man," he said, "if you weren't here right now, I'd be in my silks, drinking a nice holiday liqueur. Instead I have to talk about roadkill. No, I don't think you can hallucinate the absence of something. But I'm certainly trying really hard at the moment."

MISERABILISM

I went store-to-store, restaurant-to-restaurant around Logan Square, foisting my resume upon business owners that wanted nothing to do with me. I told myself not to act so glum, but the last time I went job hunting I had disappeared for a month with no memory of the lost time. I couldn't afford another mental lapse, having just blown two months at home justifying to my parents every life decision that had returned me to their doorstep.

Soon I was out of resumes and walking north on Albany to our new apartment, which was much larger than our place in Los Angeles. I still lived with Kim. I finally had my own bedroom, but after over a year spent sleeping in the living room I found the privacy intimidating.

Feeling grumpy, I ducked across the street into the neighborhood dive bar. Inside it was dark, cramped, and empty except for Kim, who was wiping down tables. I was surprised to see her. I asked what she was doing here.

"I needed a job so I got a job."

"How? You don't know anything about bartending."

"I didn't know anything about nannying either, but I did that for a year. This is significantly less pressure."

"Maybe I could be a nanny."

"Maybe you could sleep with your door closed."

"I'm working up to it."

She went behind the bar and poured me a beer. "You think because I'm the strongest physically that I'm the strongest emotionally," she said. "But really I just internalize my fears, which to the outside world is the same as not having any."

"I don't know if that's healthy," I said.

"You don't know much so I'm not worried. Anyway, it's a hell of a lot better than whatever life philosophy you're using. For instance, I can pay my rent."

BOOR(ED)

I was at a Christmas party in Lakeview and people were asking what I did for a living.

"I'm independently wealthy."

"And how do you fill your time?"

"Some philanthropy, but mostly I'm into bodybuilding. It's actually an affliction. I have horrible body dysmorphia. Probably you don't know what that's like unless there's a version where you think you're better-looking than you are."

Eventually they left me alone and I locked myself in the bathroom for a breather. My demon reflection leered back at me so I whited-out the mirror with a bar of soap. I sat at the edge of the tub and hoped my behavior was the demon's fault.

My phone rang. It was Alec, home for the week in New York.

"How's the party?"

"Not good. I'm holed up in the john."

"Me too," he said, but I already knew that. It was the only place he ever called me from. He asked about my holidays and I told him about my trip to the Upper Peninsula with my dad, recounting our afternoon-long walks in the woods, peppering my descriptions with words like grotto, inlet, gully, juniper, words I thought were evocative even if I didn't know what they meant: "The snow-caked grotto gave way to a shining inlet over which draped a translucent gully, the sweet smell of frosted juniper tickling my nose."

"Beautiful. I can picture it exactly. Meanwhile I mistimed a burrito in the city and now I'm in the toilet on the train back to Newark. Anyway, you sound upset. Lay it on me."

"The truth is, I'm in a bad way. I tried mingling but I couldn't stop insulting people. Everyone got mad, so I ducked in here. I'm trying not to be a weasel anymore but I think I've gone too far in the other direction."

He grunted. "I'll tell you what. It feels like I've got a weasel tearing its way out my asshole."

We talked for a while longer and then said goodbye and I went back to the party. I kept to the hallways and guzzled three beers, planning to get blind drunk before walking home in the cold as I didn't have any money for the bus.

I opened a fourth or fifth beer and wondered if any of these people were French. I was twenty-three years old and had never in my life talked to a French person. I was at the edge of a cliff with thoughts like these.

ON THE PHONE

I was in bed writing suggestive texts to my friends' girlfriends.

'One day,' I wrote Meredith, 'everyone will be dead and it'll finally just be you and me.'

'And almost immediately after that,' she wrote back, 'it'll just be me.'

'All I ever wanted in life,' I wrote Jeannette, 'is for someone to shave my neck hair.'

'And all I ever wanted in life,' she wrote back, 'is to be alone in a room with you and a razor.'

Mom called.

"Are you sure my Christmas gift is in the mail?" She was referring to the cell phone case I had yet to order for her.

"Yes. But now is not a great time, Mom. I'm busy."

"It's the middle of January. I'm beginning to think you're a liar. Plus my birthday is coming up in a week. You're going to be two gifts in the hole."

"Come on. You don't care about gifts. You're better than that."

"No, I'm not. I'm a real monster. Which explains how I could have raised such a disappointment."

"Who, Kim?" I looked out my window. From my mattress on the floor all I could see was the sky, dense with snow clouds, filling my room with gray, stale light. I rolled away from the wall, where a thin line of frost had gathered on the molding, where the duct tape I had used to block the cold air coming in from the electrical outlet had begun to peel away. My cup of coffee had gone frigid; that is to say, room temperature.

"I have a question: What did you even do in Los Angeles for a whole year?"

"Now you're just harassing me."

"I'm entitled."

"You know who I like? Who's a real cool person? Dad."

EVERYONE ELSE

I had the idea that if I hung around my sister's bar long enough they'd have to hire me, but what really happened is I became a regular instead.

"Man, you've got to get out of here," she said. "You're starting to blend in with everyone else, getting sentimental like everyone else. Pretty soon I'll have to start treating you like everyone else: with total disinterest and disdain."

"You could, potentially, pay me to stay away."

She fished in her pocket and gave me three dollars for a coffee. She told me to go to New Wave Coffee to use their Wi-Fi and download our movies for the week. I hated doing this. It always took like five hours. Plus, we were on a Katharine Hepburn kick and it was making me a little heartbroken. Because she was dead.

"Don't be heartbroken," Kim said. "She was probably a rich jerk like everyone else. And, I mean, what, she was in love with Spencer Tracy? Red flag right there."

"You can't judge people by who they love."

"I can judge you for saying bullshit like that. Now get out of here. I'm cutting you off."

Walking to New Wave, I thought maybe these errands would be more tolerable if I pretended to be someone else—say, my sister. So I started stomping around, kind of tensing at passersby like a big, mean dog. I started thinking Kim's thoughts. I thought about how much I liked weight-lifting, soup, and my brother. I worried about him. It seemed like all he had eaten in the past three weeks was a giant tub of Portillo's beef left over from one of our mom's work parties. He refused to throw it out even though it had clearly gone bad. He smelled like gravy all the time and had developed conjunctivitis, two things surely related.

New Wave was packed and I ended up sitting at a small table across from a preteen. I could feel him sizing me up while I turned on my laptop.

"What's your name?" he asked.

"Kim," I said.

"Me, too," he said slowly.

Great, a liar, I thought. His face was hard and chapped, and his teeth were clacking non-stop. He was only in jeans and a ratty Local H t-shirt. I pushed my coffee toward him and he took a sip. I asked where his coat was.

He shrugged and looked into the coffee. "I got home from school and my mom was sitting on the kitchen floor chain-smoking her way through a carton of cigarettes and eating a whole brick of cheddar cheese. I decided I didn't need to see any of this anymore. Like, I'm supposed to live here for six or seven more years, at least? Probably more, because I'm dumb as shit and no way I'll go to college. So I looked around and thought, you know, no thanks. Then I guess I kind of walked out without any of my stuff, like the dumb shit I am. I guess I kind of ran away."

"I could never run away when I was your age. Even when I wanted to."

"Why?"

"I had braces. I was nervous if I left home I'd never get them off."

"I wish I had braces. My teeth are all messed up." He bared them at me. He was right, they weren't pretty. He looked around the cafe. "If I had nice teeth like these people, I would at least try to dress better. Why is everyone here dressed like a shithead?"

"Welcome to adulthood," I said, then took the coffee back before he could take another sip. I didn't want to stunt his growth. "The first rule of adulthood is you're going to have to take care of yourself. Like, you have to get a job, you know. Also, you need to dress appropriately for the weather."

"'You have to take care of yourself,'" he said, mocking me in a whiny voice. "You should talk. What's wrong with your eyes? They're all slimy and crusty."

I wiped them, pulling away a long, goopy string of discharge. "This is just how they are now. I've been poisoned by the Portillo's corporation."

"It's hard to look at."

"You are, too," I said. "Your face is so chapped it looks like it's going to fall off."

His bottom lip started to quiver. He shoved his hands into his armpits. "I really wish I had brought my coat. I really, really wish I had brought my coat."

It occurred to me he had a lot on his mind, a lot more than I did, a guy a decade older. What he needed was a few hours' distraction.

"Hey man," I said. "Do you know who Katharine Hepburn is?" He sniffled and shook his head. I scooted my chair over to his side of the table and offered him one of my earbuds, then queued up *The Philadelphia Story.* "Welcome to the rest of your life."

Much later that night, I got home and ran to my room and curled in front of my space heater, hugging my legs to my chest. I told Kim I needed a steaming bowl of beef, stat. In a few minutes she came back with an apple and a blanket, which she draped over my shoulders.

"I need twenty bucks for a new jacket," I said. "Or however much a jacket costs. Don't ask. Just know that today I performed a great act of kindness." I bit into the apple. "This is better than the beef."

"I'm sorry for what I said about Katharine Hepburn earlier," she said. "Everyone should be allowed to crush on whatever movie star they want."

"Nah, man. I'm over her. I passed it on to some kid at New Wave. Kind of like the videotape in *The Ring*. It's his problem, now. Speaking of which, I downloaded a slew of horror movies. Let's get started."

"Finally," she said. "Things are getting back to normal."

FREEZE OUT

My sister couldn't get back into the apartment because the lock on the gate had frozen. "You need oil," I said. "Oil will warm it right up." I was telling her this from inside the gate, shivering in a bathrobe, my dead legs bare down to my slippers.

"We don't have any oil," she said.

"Talk to Manuel, four doors down. He has a tiny bottle. He helped me yesterday. But pass me the groceries first."

She tried, but the paper bag didn't fit through the bars.

"Did you get peanut butter?"

"Yes."

"Give me the peanut butter, at least."

"It doesn't fit."

"Then throw it over the gate," I said.

"It's the good stuff. In a glass jar. You'll drop it."

I argued but she told me to name one thing I'd caught in the past month.

I couldn't do it.

She left the groceries on the sidewalk and went four doors over to Manuel's. He was fat and old and wore a fedora. And he had cancer, which was either on the back of his neck or his spine. Maybe his ear. I didn't know. He had been vague, calling it simply "the cancer" and pointing to the general area behind his head.

120

I stayed outside to watch the bags. Of course, if some-one wanted to steal them I couldn't do anything. If it came to it, I'd ask them to at least leave the peanut butter. It was the natural kind and most people didn't like that stuff. Kim liked it enough but didn't know how to use it. She never bothered mixing and after one serving the jar was ruined. It was on me to get to it first and do it right.

After a few minutes she came back, not with Manuel but with his daughter Paz. Paz was twenty-eight and owned the house where she and Manuel lived. Some-times she hung out at Kim's bar where she was known to go around trying to light the coasters on fire. She had a shaved head and big teeth. When she closed her mouth it looked like she was holding in a yell, or a small bird or rat. Kim once told me the way to get anyone to make out with you was to send gigantic coming-in-hot gamma thought-beams in their direction. If the cancer wasn't hereditary Paz would have it soon anyway because I was irradiating her.

"Where's Manuel?" I asked.

"He's sleeping. Not well. It's hard for him to get up. He's like a turtle."

"How's his... the back of his head?"

She frowned at me, then held the tiny bottle of oil to the keyhole and squeezed it. "Now try."

Kim put the key in the hole and it turned. Across the street, a middle-aged lady swept the thinnest layer of snow off her sidewalk with a plain old broom. It was getting harder and harder for me not to yell when I saw things like that. People mamby-pambied around lunatics, but you couldn't let them do whatever they wanted. She needed to know: let the snow accumulate, then use a shovel. For now, strike it from your mind. Go inside. Have a warm drink. Put on some Django Reinhardt. A pair of slippers, a bathrobe.

Kim, who knew about my thought-beams for Paz, picked up the groceries and slipped through the gate and into the apartment, to let me take a stab at it:

"Do you want to come in?"

"No."

A WIN

I was on my bed modeling my new black boots for myself while Kim sat on the weight bench doing arm curls.

"Are you wearing my shoes?" Kim asked.

"No. These are mine," I said. "In what hell do you think we have the same sized feet?"

"The same one where I can bench more than you." She let the barbells clank to the floor, then got on her back and grunted out ten reps.

"You can't bench more than me," I said.

"Then...*unh!*...prove it...*unh!*...pussy."

I had found the bench and a bucket of weights in the alley under an official-looking sign that said something about rats I didn't read too closely. With a little duct-tape the bench was useable, but wobbly.

"You want to know how I know you're a psychopath? You have a weight bench in your bedroom," Kim told me.

Two weeks later she was on it every day. I didn't mind. My room was freezing and I needed any heat source I could find. The temperature jumped about ten degrees when she worked out.

She sat up and rolled her neck until it cracked, then stepped aside and ushered me to the bench. I took hold of the bar.

"Oh wait," I said. "This is incredibly easy." I pumped out ten reps, then another ten, then I started kind of lobbing the bar into the air and catching it at my chest. Kim looked upset.

"We're not in hell yet," I said.

BARF FLY

On the first mild day of the year I picked up my friend Meredith from the Logan Square L stop. We had gone to high school and college together, but apart from a blurry wedding in December I hadn't seen her in over a year. Now she was in town from Washington, DC, to see a German puppet show with her parents in Naperville, which seemed about right. In the meantime she was staying with me.

"For a while—do you want to hear about this?—for a while I was pursuing this twenty-eight-year-old who lives four doors down with her parents," I said. "But she wasn't having it. She turned out to be super Catholic and said I wasn't spiritual enough. That's the word she used, 'spiritual.' Not spiritual enough? I have the transplanted legs of a dead man and the last girl I saw put a demon inside me. That's more Catholic than anything she's done, I bet. *Spiritual.* I need an exorcism, I'm so spiritual."

She wouldn't stop laughing. "You seem jittery."

"It's all these icicles melting. All the dripping." I stomped through a puddle. "How's your life?"

"Golden. I have a job, a boyfriend, and friends in other cities. I am floating through life."

"Must be nice."

"Give me a break."

I wrestled her backpack away from her. "Did you bring me anything?"

We dumped her stuff at my place then went to Kim's bar. Paz was there, in the corner, trying to light a cardboard coaster on fire. As a whole it wouldn't catch so she started ripping it into little strips, knotting them into kindling.

"That's not very Catholic of you," I yelled.

"Who are you shouting at?" Meredith said.

"That's her," I said. "She's here. Who knew?"

"You, probably," Kim said. "Your friend here has turned into a weird guy and not in an OK way," she told Meredith. "I thought I trained him better than that." She poured Meredith a beer but not me. At the moment we weren't talking. I recently realized she had been feeding me lies about celebrity deaths. As the one of us who used the Internet, she was my gatekeeper for that stuff. ("You should be grateful," she had said. "Most people never think someone is dead and then find out they're still alive. I gave you a unique emotional experience, maybe the only unique one you've ever had.") Still, I wanted a beer and I smacked the bar repeatedly until she gave me one. Then I had eight or nine more. Paz burnt the coaster to embers and I wanted to say something to her, mostly so I could call her 'Zap,' the cute nickname I would've used had we grown serious.

"'Spaz' would work, too," Meredith said.

"What?"

"As a cute nickname or whatever, for that girl," she said. She pinched the bridge of her nose. "Jesus. I make myself sick." We slumped over the bar. Kim's shift had ended hours ago. She got off early sometimes to do interviews or cover shows for a bunch of websites and local papers. I don't know. Kim Steele, writer-bartender. She was doing great.

"So maybe I'm not spiritual," I told Meredith as Zap blew the ashes into the air. "But remember that summer in college when we ate fifty-cent ice cream cones and had that cooler of mini Coronas and used my dad's projector to watch outdoor movies on a sheet against the garage? *Jackass? Jackass 1.5? Jackass 2? Jackass 3?* If I die and somehow fail to cease to exist, I hope I go back to that. I hope I'm a ghost, hovering behind our lawn chairs, wisping against our necks…"

"Which is the one where they set up a miniature town and there's a green hill overlooking it but really it's a painted butt and then he has diarrhea?" Meredith asked.

"*Jackass 3*," I said.

ONE LEFT

We were at our parents' house, not on purpose. Every time I drove us anywhere at night, we ended up in their driveway. It had been going on all week. No matter where we wanted to go, we always found ourselves here.

"This never happens when I drive," Kim said.

"You never drive."

"Well, it wouldn't happen if I did. Going home to our parents' house every night? This is distinctly a *you* problem."

We went inside and yelled at the pile of blankets that was our mom.

"It happened again," Kim said. "We're home. Wake up."

The blankets stirred, then yawned.

"Come out from under there," Kim said. She tugged on the blankets, but Mom held them in place.

"Get away," the blankets said. "Leave me alone."

"Excuse us?"

"You're ghosts or ghouls or something. I know this is a trick. Every night you come in here and try to get me to take the blankets off. Well, I won't do it. My kids live in the city. They wouldn't come home every night just to harass me. I mean, maybe they would, but they can't afford the gas."

Kim had a theory that our apartment was low on supplies, so it kept sending us to La Grange to get more stuff. That couldn't have been the answer. A week had passed since the problem started and we had cleaned out our parents' reserves of paper towels, toilet paper, tissue paper, food, light bulbs, laundry detergent, end tables, etcetera. But it kept happening.

"Maybe it's this deep fryer," Kim said. We were in the kitchen. "Maybe it'll stop if we take the deep fryer."

I told Kim I thought maybe we kept getting sent back here to spend quality time with our parents.

"But why?"

"Maybe they're going to be dead soon."

"That's ridiculous," Kim said. "We'll be dead long before them. They're safe here. We're the ones being driven crazy. Even now, I feel like we're coming up on the end. Because what's on the other side of all this stuff? All this garbage that happens to us? Certainly not a normal life." She gestured at me to pick up the fryer. I followed her out to the car and put it in the backseat.

We were on the highway, almost to the California Avenue exit. The curse seemed to be broken. We were going to make it.

"Tomorrow," Kim said, "me and you are going out."

"I'd rather not. I have plans. I'm going to sort through all the underwear I stole from Dad. A lot of the pairs are in shreds, or have holes blown out the backside."

"No. Tomorrow me and you are going out. We're going to get rowdy. We're going to pack it in."

"Do you mean we're going to do a lot of fun stuff, or kill ourselves?"

"If you try to back out, or do that thing where you let me out-drink you and then ditch me, then at the very least I'll kill you."

"I won't ditch you," I said. "I would never ditch you."

"Well, good. So we'll go out, have a good time, and then it will be over," she said, pulling into a parking spot on our street.

"What do you mean, over?" I asked.

She didn't answer. I looked up.

We were back in our parents' driveway.

FUCK AND RUN

I was feeling vulnerable in a corner booth at a bar after several beers and a plate of nachos I had ordered "for the table," even though I was alone. I held my phone to my nose and sniffed it like you might a love letter delivered by horseback to a windswept cattle ranch in the 1800s. Laurie had sent me a text. She was back in the States, broke, and living above her aunt's garage outside Traverse City, working on some poems about dead timber barons, which centered around baron/barren wordplay:

'not going well but i get to stay in bed or the woods all day. and aunt lucille has a rose-pink cadillac she lets me take to town where i sometimes try to scope a paul newman hudtype though most men here are over sixty-five or wearing camo overalls. thinking i might pack it in and buy a pick-up, take it down to LA, but then that's a neil young song and i already did that.'

And so on. I pinched the last nacho crumbs and dropped them into my mouth. It was Friday night. The place milled with limbs, heads, and torsos, none of which were connected to each other. Too many kids in this tub. I tried to look like I was waiting for someone.

A moan at the bar.

Two guys with big tummies and shaggy mustaches, one helping the other, shuffled their way to my booth.

"Do you mind?" they asked.

"Not at all," I said.

They sat down with an exhale. The one on the right was sweating. He lifted his leg under the table and propped it next to me.

"Gout," he said.

"Would you mind untying his shoelace to relieve the pressure?" the other asked.

He winced and smacked the table like I was ripping out stitches. We ordered more beers. They were middle-aged brothers from Milwaukee but didn't give any reason for being in Chicago, and as the hours passed, my sense of place beyond the booth grew unsteady. I had a vision of being bound and gagged along with Laurie in the back of Neil Young's truck, barreling west through Utah.

"Milwaukee is easy living, up until the end," they said. "By that we mean our mother owned a roadside bar for thirty years and only at the end did she get sent away for false tax returns. That's not so bad. They've got her in that correctional center downtown for a little while, so we're on a visit."

"I have a cousin who works in the Sears Tower," I said. "Sixty-seventh floor. She can see the inmates playing volleyball from her office."

"That really true?" This was upsetting to them. Nobody forces their mother to play sports. They started talking about tying bedsheets together.

I said if I had known they were coming I would have saved some nachos. "Or, are nachos bad for gout?"

He wiped his eyes. "If you're making them right."

A tap on the shoulder. Kevin With Security wanted to let me know my friend had fallen over on the sidewalk and they weren't going to let her in. I had come alone but said OK and gathered my things.

"You two know what a vow of poverty is?"

They nodded knowingly.

"It'll be a big tab. I had two jugs of margaritas before you showed up."

"We have places we can charge it."

Kim was out front doing ballet for the bouncers to prove she was all right. She stumbled and fell backwards against a tree, then curtsied. I had ditched her five blocks away but somehow she found me.

We walked toward the L stop, then kept walking.

"You're my own, personal…"

"…Jesus?"

"Zombie. I can't get away," I said. "Slowly but surely you'll eat me alive."

"I knew it. It's happening." Earlier we had fought because, in anticipation of Alec and Jeannette visiting from LA in a few weeks, she had warned me I might get confused and want to move back. Way off-base. It was draining to walk around a city thinking vaguely about how you should go on some auditions, see what happens. The ocean and mountains were nice but made me suspicious that I was being distracted. But then, that was my problem. Truly, I didn't have a stake in the argument one way or another, but sometimes you have to fight. Anyway, I liked it here, where the weirdos didn't try so hard.

"Someone got famous in this neighborhood," Kim said. "I can't remember. Either Liz Phair or Gacy." She bumped her shoulder off a brick wall and the conversation took a leap. "What I need is, give me a swan song."

"Me, personally? Like you want me to kill you?"

"If somebody has to." It gave me a sick empty feeling. I was eighty years old alone in a studio apartment looking down at the street on a Saturday night. I hadn't seen her in years and that would be true forever. Then she belched and laughed and said she'd cleared some room. We circled the neighborhood back to where we started and Kevin With Security decided to be forgiving and let us inside. A big mistake. I felt a little better. We could trick at least one person into thinking we weren't a total disaster. Kim and I looked at each other, smugly. No one had any idea what was coming.

PHOTO BY DANIELLE DUFF

ABOUT THE AUTHOR

This is T. Sean Steele's first book. Find him at tseansteele.com.

@unnamedpress

f

facebook.com/theunnamedpress

t

unnamedpress.tumblr.com

un

www.unnamedpress.com

@unnamedpress

7-31-18
8-12-21
    13(LHQ)
    JUL 3 1 2018